Stories for 1 Year Olds

Stories for 1 Year Olds

LITTLE TIGER PRESS
London

Contents

Who's That Scratching at My Door?

Amanda Leslie

hmmmm !

8

I wish I had a real friend to play with . . .

grrrowl !

What's that noise?

Who's
that
growling
at my
door?

A big brown bear!

grrrowl!!

grrrowl!!

You are far too big
to play with me!

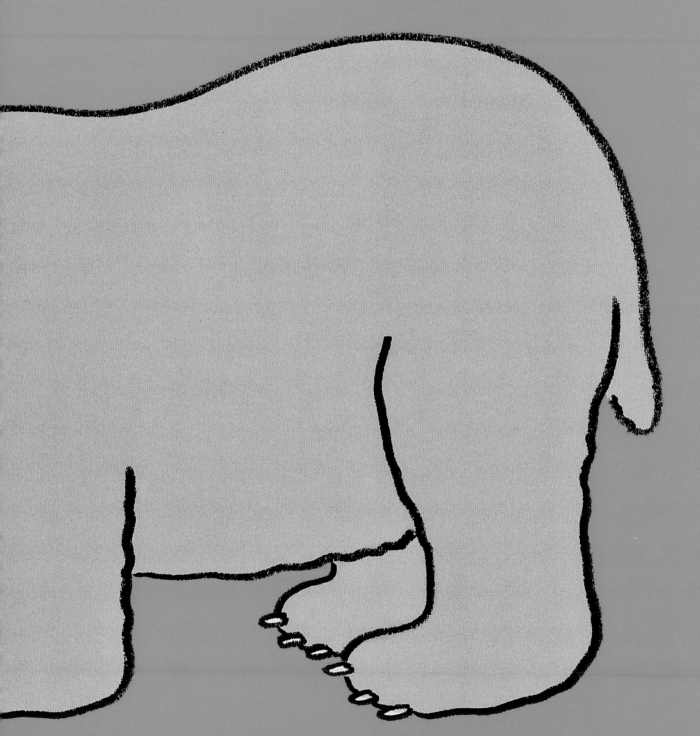

Who's
that
munching
at my
door?

A tall orange giraffe!

munch!

munch!

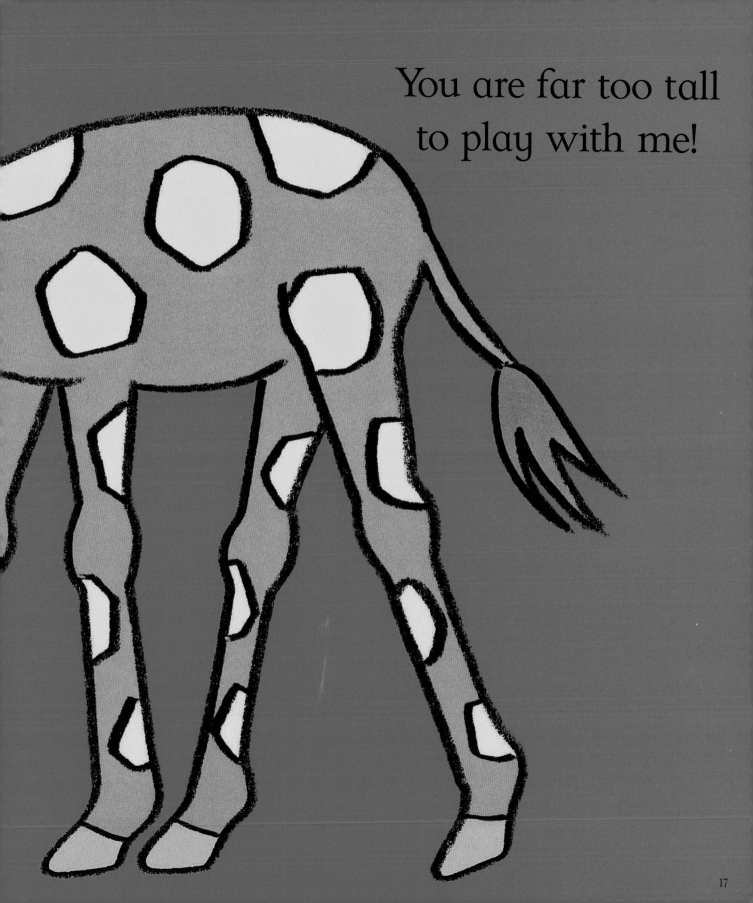

You are far too tall
to play with me!

Who's that croaking at my door?

A slimy
green
frog!

croak!

You are far too slimy
to play with me!

croak!

Who's that giggling at my door?

A naughty red monkey!

hee hee ha ha!

You are far too naughty
to play with me!

ha ha hee hee!

Who's that scratching and sniffing at my door?

A sniffy,
licky,
cuddly
puppy!

Scratch!

Scratch!

Hooray!
You're just right for me.
Come in and play!

My Little Baby

Monday's Child

Monday's child is fair of face,

Tuesday's child is full of grace,

Wednesday's child is full of woe,

Thursday's child has far to go,

Friday's child is loving and giving,

Saturday's child works hard for a living,

But the child that's born on the Sabbath day

Is bonny, blithe, good and gay.

Ten Tiny Fingers

Ten tiny fingers, ten tiny toes,

Two chubby cheeks and one tiny nose,

Two little eyes and two little ears,

One little baby, sweet and dear!

Baby

Where did you come from, baby dear?

Out of the everywhere into here.

Where did you get those eyes so blue?

Out of the sky as I came through.

What makes the light in them sparkle and spin?

Some of the starry twinkles left in.

Where did you get that little tear?

I found it waiting when I got here.

What makes your forehead so smooth and high?

A soft hand stroked it as I went by.

What makes your cheek like a warm white rose?

I saw something better than any one knows.

~ George MacDonald

Little Friend

Katie Cook   Colleen McKeown

As Laura walked along one day,
she heard a tiny noise . . .

It was a little duckling,
shivering in the grass.

Laura sat by him, quiet
and still, until he wasn't
scared any more.

She carried him home
and cuddled him warm.

But day after day,
the duckling lay still.

"Please get better,"
Laura pleaded. She
nursed him gently . . .

until at last he was
well and impatient
to be outside.

All through the winter
they marched in the snow,
Laura and her brave little duckling.

The duckling grew strong as the days grew warmer. He wanted to swim in the spring sunshine.

"Not too far," said Laura. She was scared he'd swim right away from her.

But he didn't. He came back.
"I love you, Little Friend,"
she said.

"Will you always be
happy with me?"

All evening she hugged him tight, as
the wild ducks called.

"You want to be with them, don't you,
Little Friend?" Laura whispered.

"I think I'll have to teach you how to fly . . .

. . . somehow!"

"Let's run with the wind!" Laura laughed.

"Faster and faster . . ."

". . . you can do it!" she cried.

"You can fly!"

He looked so beautiful.

"Come back soon," Laura whispered.

"I'll never forget you, my brave little friend."

Love You, Baby

All My Love

A baby squeeze,
A little hug,
A BIG, BIG kiss,
And all my love!

Baby Wonder

Baby blink,
Baby smile,
Baby sleep –
For a while!
Baby walk,
Baby run –
What a wonder
You've become!

Baby Love

I love your button nose

and your chubby little chin,

The dimples in your cheeks

and your cheeky-monkey grin.

I love your sunny smile

and your bonny, baby giggle,

The toddle in your walk

as you wibble-wobble-wiggle.

The words you say so well

and the ones you often muddle.

But most of all, the thing I love

is giving you a cuddle.

Little Bunny's Bathtime

Jane Johnson

Gaby Hansen

"Bathtime for my bunnies!"
called Mrs Rabbit, and her
children all came running.
All except her youngest
little bunny.

"I don't want a bath,"
said Little Bunny.
"I want to go on playing."

"You really want to play all by
yourself?" asked his mummy.
Little Bunny nodded, but
now he wasn't so sure.

"Well, you be good while
I'm busy with the others,"
said Mrs Rabbit, plopping
them into the water.

"Swish, swash, swoosh," sang
the little rabbits happily, swirling
their bubbles into a heap.
  Little Bunny wanted
to play too.

"Look at me!" he called,
hiding behind the towels.

"Yes, dear," said Mrs Rabbit, but
she went on washing the others.
   "Tickly, wickly, wiggle toes," giggled
her little bunnies, waggling their
feet in the water.

"Guess where I am!"
shouted Little Bunny,
hidden in the linen
basket.

"Found you," smiled his
mother, lifting the lid . . .

But she turned back
to finish washing
the others.

"Up you come!" puffed Mrs Rabbit,
lifting her children out of the tub.

"Rub-a-dub-dub, you've all had a scrub!"
she laughed. "What lovely clean
bunnies you are!"

Little Bunny was cross.
He wanted his mummy
to notice him.

So he
climbed
up . . .

and up — as far
as he could.
But suddenly...

SPLOSH!

He fell into the bath!

"Oh my!" said Mrs Rabbit, fishing
him out straight away.

Little Bunny gazed up at her happily.

"I'm ready for a bath now, Mummy,"
he said, smiling sweetly.

Mrs Rabbit couldn't
help smiling back.
"Off you go and play
quietly," she said to
the others.

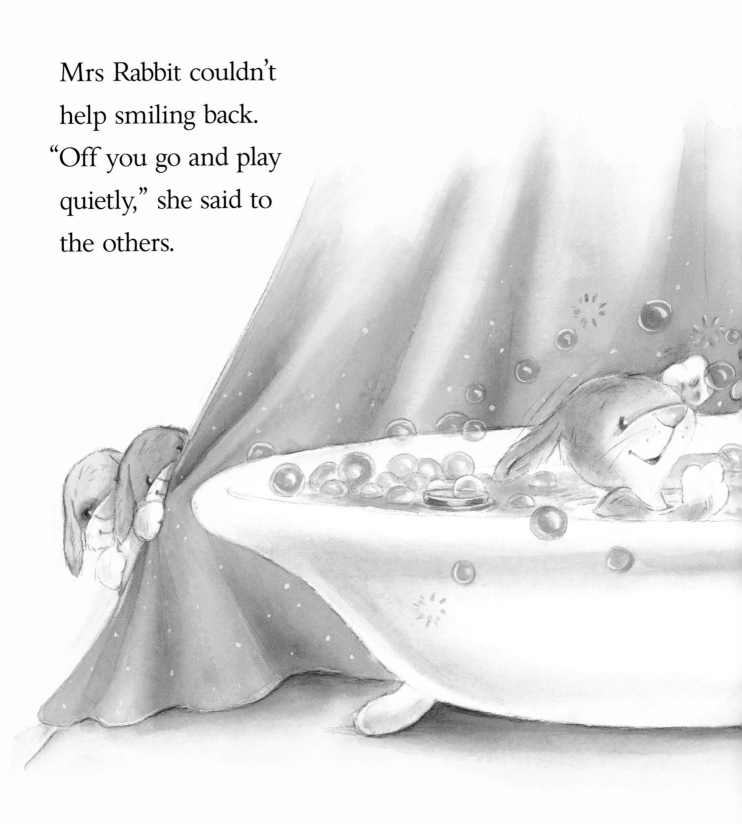

Then she ran
fresh water and gave
Little Bunny a bath —
all to himself.

She dried his fur
and whiskers, and said,
"Ooh, you smell
so clean and nice!"

And Little Bunny kissed his mummy
and hugged her tight.

"There now, all done," sighed Mrs Rabbit.
"It's time for bed. Where are my other
little bunnies?"

She found them in the kitchen.

"Oh no! What a mess!" cried
Mrs Rabbit. "You're dirty again!
You all need another bath!"

"Yes," giggled Little Bunny.
"All except me!"

It's Playtime!

Shall We Go Dancing?

Shall we go dancing round the moon
and wave our arms up high?
Or shall we go tip-toe on the stars
then leap across the sky?
Shall we go to the ocean floor
and stamp our feet like this,
Then twist and turn and tumble
with the spinning, dancing fish?
Shall I lift baby up-and-up,
then round and round we go?
Come nestle safely in my arms -
I'll rock you to-and-fro.

Come Out to Play

Come out to play - it's nearly 1.
Bring your teddy and join the fun.
Come out to play - it's nearly 2.
You say, "Hide," and I'll say, "Boo!"
Come out to play - it's nearly 3.
Over the hill and up the tree.
Come out to play - it's nearly 4.
One last game, but we want more!
At 5 we'll head for home, but then
Tomorrow we can play again!

Lavender's Blue

Lavender's blue, dilly dilly,
Lavender's green,
When I am king, dilly dilly,
You shall be queen.

What Are You Doing in My Bed?

David Bedford   Daniel Howarth

Kip the kitten had nowhere to sleep
on a dark and cold winter's night.
So he crept through a door . . .

. . . and curled up warm and
snug in somebody's bed.

Then out of the dark,
Kip heard . . .

whispers and hisses,
and soft feet padding
through the night.
Bright green eyes peered
in through the window,
and suddenly . . .

. . . one, two, three, four, five, six cats
came banging through the cat door!
They tumbled and skidded and rolled
across the floor, where they found . . .

. . . Kip!

"What are YOU doing in OUR bed?"

shouted the six angry cats.

"Your bed?" said Kip.
"But this bed's too small for you.
 You'd never all fit!"
  "Never fit?" said the cats.
"Just you watch . . ."

One, two, three cats curled up
neatly, head to tail . . .
then four, five, six cats
piled on top.

"See? There's no room
for you," they said.
"You'd never fit."
    "Never fit?"
said Kip.
"Just you
    watch . . ."

Tottering and teetering,
Kip carefully climbed on top.
"I'll sleep here," he said.
    "OK," the cats yawned.
"But don't fidget or snore."
    And they fell asleep in a heap.
        But suddenly, a big, deep,
growly voice said . . .

"WHAT ARE YOU DOING IN MY BED? SCRAM!"

The cats skitter-skattered round the room, but they only found hard, cold places to sleep.

Harry the dog was comfy in his bed,

and he soon began to snore.

But then an icy wind whistled in

through the cat door, and Harry

awoke and shivered.

Kip whispered, "Follow me . . ."
and he quickly led six cold cats
across the floor . . .

. . . to the cosy bed.
"We'll keep you warm,"
said Kip.

"You'll never all fit," chattered Harry.

"Never fit?" said Kip. "Just you watch . . ."

Kip and Harry snored right through the night under their warm blanket of cats.

And they all fitted purr-fectly!

It's Fun to Be One

When You Were One

When you were one,
You were still so new.
But we couldn't imagine
Our life without you!

What Shall We Eat?

Baby, Baby,
What shall we eat?
Some carrots or peas,
Or peaches so sweet?
Baby, Baby,
Look under there!
Your food's on the floor,
It's under your chair!

Bathtime

Splish, splash,
Time for a bath!
Soap and bubbles,
Clean at last!

The Hippo

A hippo got stuck in a washing machine,
Now the clothes are all muddy,
but Hippo is clean!

Goodnight
PiggyWiggy

Diane and Christyan Fox

At night-time when it's dark outside, I lie in bed and think of all the things

I'd like to be when I grow up...

I'd like to be
a fearless
fireman...
coming to the

rescue.

Or I could be
a brave
pilot...

looping the loop high above

the clouds.

Or perhaps a caring doctor...

making people well again.

Or what about a digger driver...

digging
down,
deep
into the
ground?

Or even a racing

speedy driver...

zooming around the track.

Or maybe a clever chef...

making
a big,
yummy
cake.

But most of all
I'd like to be a
daring pirate,
sailing the
seven seas...

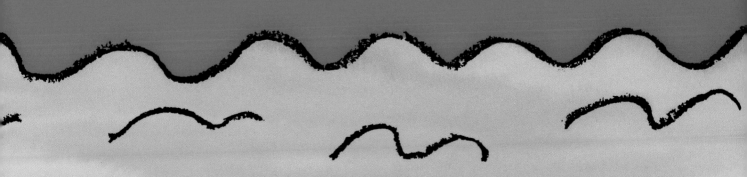

I wonder who I'll be tomorrow?

Goodnight Teddy, sweet dreams.

Time for Bed

Where Does Baby Sleep?

A bear snores soundly in its den,

A bird sleeps in its nest.

But for a baby just like you,

A cosy bed is best!

Hush Now, Sleepyhead

Hush now, sleepyhead,

Lay down in your bed.

Sweet dreams all night through,

Big kiss, I love you!

Sleep, Baby, Sleep

Sleep, baby, sleep.

Your father guards the sheep.

Your mother shakes the dreamland tree,

Down falls a little dream for thee.

Sleep, baby, sleep.

Night-Night, Poppy!

Claire Freedman

Jane Massey

It was bedtime, but Poppy couldn't find her favourite bear, Growly Ted. She'd looked everywhere.

Mummy had to tuck her in
with Quacky Duck instead.

"Night-night, Poppy, night-night,
Quacky Duck," said Mummy.

"Night-night, Mummy and
Quacky Duck," said Poppy.

"Quack-quack!" quacked
Quacky Duck.

Poppy would have fallen fast
asleep right then. But OH NO!
The bed didn't feel quite right.

So Poppy went to find Furry Cat.

"Night-night, Quacky Duck and Furry Cat,"
said Poppy.

"Miaow," purred Furry Cat.

"Quack-quack," quacked Quacky Duck.

Poppy would have fallen fast asleep that
very minute. But OH NO! The bed STILL
didn't feel quite right. It felt too empty.

Out Poppy climbed to look for Hooty Owl.

"Night-night," Poppy told Hooty Owl, Furry Cat and Quacky Duck.

"Too-whit, too-whoo," hooted Hooty Owl.

"Miaow," purred Furry Cat.

"Quack-quack," quacked Quacky Duck. "Quack!"

Poppy would have fallen asleep in a flash.

But OH NO! Now the bed felt too draughty.

Where had Dimple Dog got to?

Poppy found him downstairs, behind the curtains.

"Night-night, Dimple Dog and
Hooty Owl," said Poppy.
"Night-night, Furry Cat and
Quacky Duck."
    "Woof-woof," barked Dimple Dog.
    "Too-whit, too-whoo," hooted
Hooty Owl.
    "Miaow," purred Furry Cat.
    Quacky Duck didn't say a word.
He was already fast asleep.

Poppy would have fallen fast asleep too.

But OH NO! Now the bed covers felt too loose.

Poppy crept out to find Woolly Lamb.

"Night-night, everyone," said Poppy.

"Baa-baa," bleated Woolly Lamb.

"Woof-woof," barked Dimple Dog.

"Too-whit, too-whoo," hooted Hooty Owl.

"Miaow," purred Furry Cat.

"Quack-quack," quacked Quacky Duck, who'd woken up again with all the noise.

Now Poppy would have fallen fast
asleep in an instant. But OH NO!
She just couldn't get comfy.
The pillow felt all lumpy.
  "What's under here?" said Poppy.
"Oh, so that's where you've been
hiding, silly Growly Ted!"

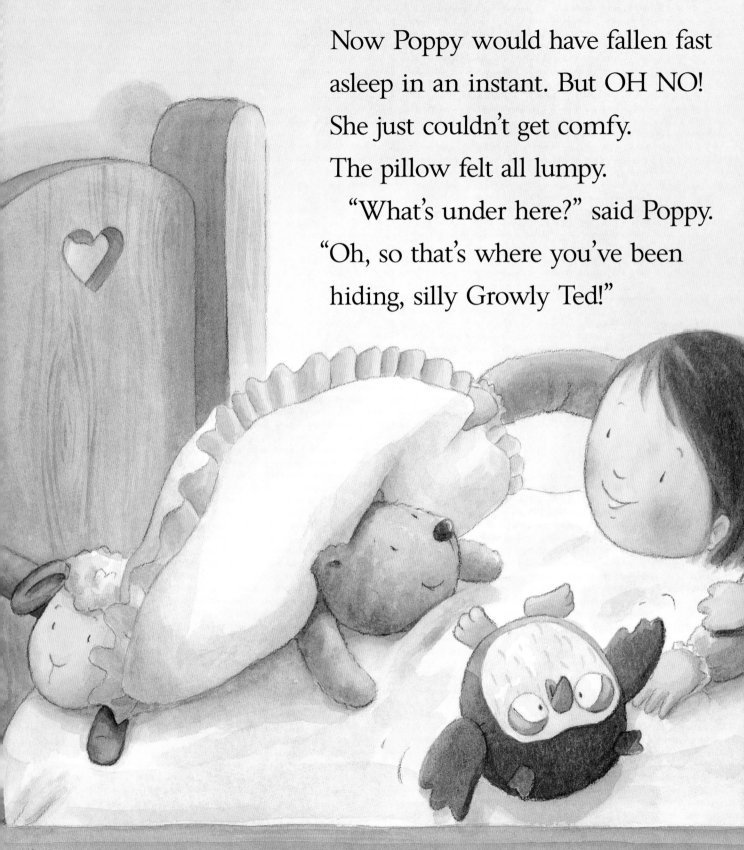

163

Then Poppy put
Quacky Duck
back in the toy box.

She propped
Furry Cat back
up on his shelf.

She put Hooty Owl
back under
the bed.

And she carried
Dimple Dog
and Woolly Lamb
back downstairs.

Then Poppy and Growly Ted settled
down together under the covers.

"Night-night, Growly Ted,"
yawned Poppy.

"Grrr!" growled Growly Ted.

And Poppy fell fast asleep.
OH YES! Because the bed felt
just right.

And Growly Ted
would have fallen fast asleep
that same second too.
But OH NO! . . .

Suddenly the bed
was far too full!
"Grrrr!"

STORIES FOR 1 YEAR OLDS

LITTLE TIGER PRESS
1 The Coda Centre
189 Munster Road
London SW6 6AW
www.littletiger.co.uk

First published in Great Britain 2013

Printed in China

LTP/1800/1063/1114

ISBN 978-1-84895-728-2

4 6 8 10 9 7 5 3

ACKNOWLEDGEMENTS

'Hush Now, Sleepyhead' by Stephanie Stansbie, copyright © Little Tiger Press 2008;
'When You Were One' by Stephanie Stansbie, copyright © Little Tiger Press 2011;
'Baby Wonder', 'Baby Love', 'Shall We Go Dancing?', 'Come Out to Play'
by Stephanie Stansbie, copyright © Little Tiger Press 2013;
'Ten Tiny Fingers', 'What Shall We Eat?', 'Bathtime', 'Where Does Baby Sleep?'
by Mara Alperin, copyright © Little Tiger Press 2011;
'All My Love', 'The Hippo' by Mara Alperin, copyright © Little Tiger Press 2013

Additional artwork by Rachel Baines, copyright © Little Tiger Press 2010, 2013

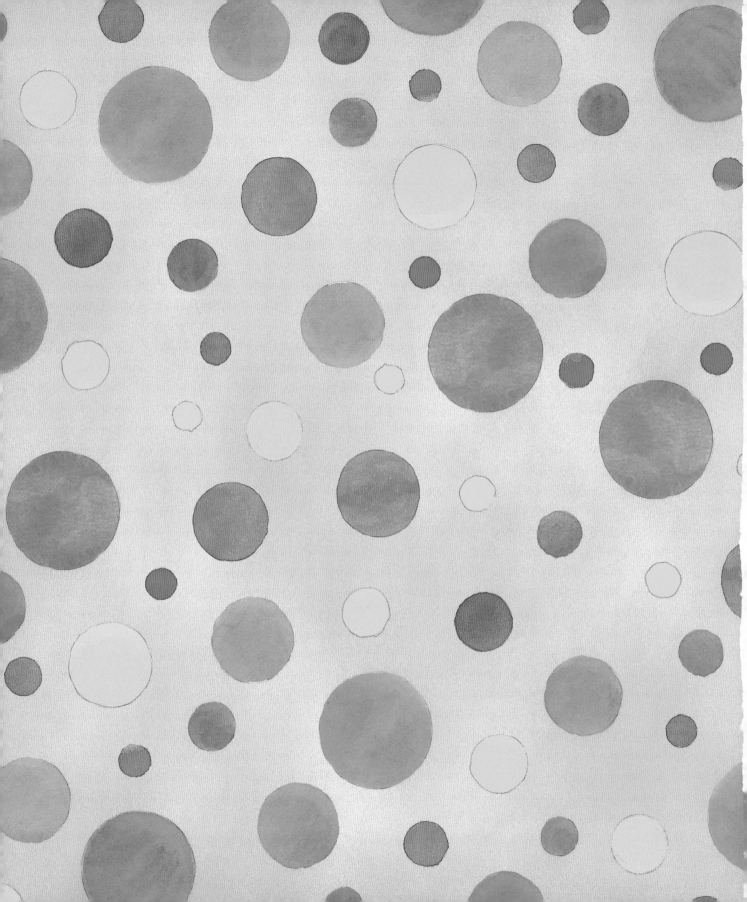